Miloš Macourek is one of Czechoslovakia's most celebrated writers. His work includes a number of screenplays (mainly comedies), and scripts for the avant-garde theatre in Prague as well as for cartoon and puppet films. He is also a distinguished poet, and his poetic and satiric imagination can be seen at work in all his writings — as in this collection for young children in which he offers a number of gently cautionary tales, told with a reckless disregard for the laws of science and of the adult world.

Marie Burg is particularly well known for her translations of folk-tales and children's stories from Czechoslovakia. Born and brought up in Prague, she came before the last war to live in England, teaching and writing French and German texts for schools. She is also the author of general books on England and Czechoslovakia for young people, as well as a contributor to British journals and broadcasting.

Adolf Born has won a number of international awards for his work as an illustrator and graphic artist. Apart from his many contributions to books he has worked on more than fifty animated films, several of them in collaboration with his fellow-Czech and great friend Miloš Macourek. He has been specially commissioned to illustrate this edition of Macourek's *Curious Tales*.

Curious tales

Miloš Macourek

Curious tales

translated from the Czech by Marie Burg
illustrated by Adolf Born

Oxford New York Toronto Melbourne
OXFORD UNIVERSITY PRESS 1980

Oxford University Press, Walton Street, Oxford OX2 6DP

OXFORD LONDON GLASGOW
NEW YORK TORONTO MELBOURNE WELLINGTON
KUALA LUMPUR SINGAPORE JAKARTA HONG KONG TOKYO
DELHI BOMBAY CALCUTTA MADRAS KARACHI
NAIROBI DAR ES SALAAM CAPE TOWN

British Library Cataloguing in Publication Data
Macourek, Miloš
   Curious tales
    I. Title II. Burg, Marie
   891.8'6'35F PG5038.M/ 78–41180
ISBN 0–19–271427–9

Printed in Great Britain by
Fakenham Press Limited
Fakenham, Norfolk

Contents

The kitchen-sink opera

A kitchen sink is an ordinary thing, but it's very important. It supplies water for pots, buckets, glasses, and watering-cans, and for baths too. In fact it supplies water from morning till night; but it really doesn't mind doing this at all. You see, whenever it has just a bit of free time, it begins to sing. True, there are kitchen sinks who can't sing very well, and some who sing quite out of tune – not everybody can be the world's greatest talent, after all. But just imagine – in one kitchen there was a sink who sang so beautifully that, whenever he sang, the clock actually stopped ticking – she was so carried away.

The sink had a marvellous voice, as deep as a wash-tub. In the evening, when the washing-up was done and the whole house was quiet, he began to sing little songs such as *There's a Hole in My Bucket*. And the glasses, the pots, the plates, and even the clock listened, not daring to move or even breathe. The songs were so lovely that they all had to smile, whether they felt like it or not. It was so beautiful.

But one evening when the sink was singing, a couple of old kitchen chairs began to creak furiously: 'Pipe down! That's enough! They're singing *Noah's Flood* on TV – we

1

want to watch.' They just wouldn't stop creaking.

What could the kitchen sink do? He stopped singing and he didn't make a sound, but he was sad. One after another, his tears began to drip. Finally, one red saucepan couldn't control himself any longer, and he said: 'Those chairs ought to be ashamed of themselves. Can't a sink have a sing after his work is done?'

'In fact,' said the kitchen cupboard, 'why should the

2

sink waste his time here at all?' And, as he was facing the sink anyway, he told him straight: 'Don't be a fool! You're wasted here. You'd do better to go to music school. Who knows, one day you might even get into the opera!'

The sink thought it over, and in the end he said to himself: 'Why shouldn't I learn to sing? Perhaps I really have a talent.' So he picked himself up and left.

The music school was full of singing everywhere, with a piano playing here, a clarinet piping there. It all made the sink quite nervous, but anyway he went up the stairs, right into the principal's room.

'I am the kitchen sink,' he introduced himself as he went in.

The principal rose to his feet, saying: 'Pleased to meet you.' And, as he happened to be thirsty, he turned on the tap to fill a glass with water from the sink.

'I'd like to learn singing,' said the sink. 'People say I've got talent. The glasses and the pots, the cupboard, and even the clock say so.'

'What the glasses and the pots say doesn't carry any weight with me,' the principal replied. 'Try and sing something, then we'll see.'

So the sink cleared his throat-pipe and began to sing *There's a Hole in My Bucket*. It really was so wonderful that the principal had to smile, whether he felt like it or not. It was so beautiful. In the end he said: 'Indeed, you've talent, you ought to go far. You're accepted. Just behave yourself and, above all, don't make any puddles.'

And so the sink screwed his tap down tight and began to study and study, and he learned to sing all the scales and all the songs and all the operas. When he had mastered it all, he picked himself up and went to the opera house down by the river.

The opera house was full of singing, with a men's choir here, a women's choir over there, and a children's choir as well. But the sink wasn't nervous at all, for he was used to this by now. He went straight to the director, and sang about twelve to fifteen operas for him.

'Right,' said the director at last. 'I'm very pleased to take you on, because the sink we have at the moment can't sing. And you know yourself how bad it looks to have a kitchen sink at the opera who can't sing a single note.'

And so he got a job – as the opera house kitchen sink. It goes without saying that he was very disappointed, and he wished a thousand times that he could go back to his own kitchen.

But just imagine! One day there was a catastrophe. The singer who took the part of Noah in *Noah's Flood* had the hiccups. Everybody was desperate, the time for the beginning of the performance drew nearer and nearer, nobody knew what was going to happen – until suddenly the director remembered the kitchen sink who could sing.

So the sink was dressed up in a long coat and fitted up with a wig, and then he was dragged on to the stage. The audience were delighted. Everybody clapped, shouting: 'This *is* a different Noah! He's got a real flood going!'

Soon the whole town was full of it. And when the two old kitchen chairs heard the news they put on red plush gowns and went to the theatre, where they saw lots of other chairs, all wearing red plush; a great number of chairs, all perfectly still. Only the two old kitchen chairs kept creaking, so that everybody could overhear them telling each other: 'It's our sink who used to sing in the kitchen. We always said he would go far.'

4

But the other chairs weren't interested. 'Could you kindly stop creaking?' they whispered. 'We'd like to hear the kitchen sink sing.'

What could the two silly old kitchen chairs do? They had to keep silent. And in that silence you could hear the kitchen sink singing; and he sang so splendidly that everyone there was carried away and they had to smile, whether they felt like it or not. It was so beautiful.

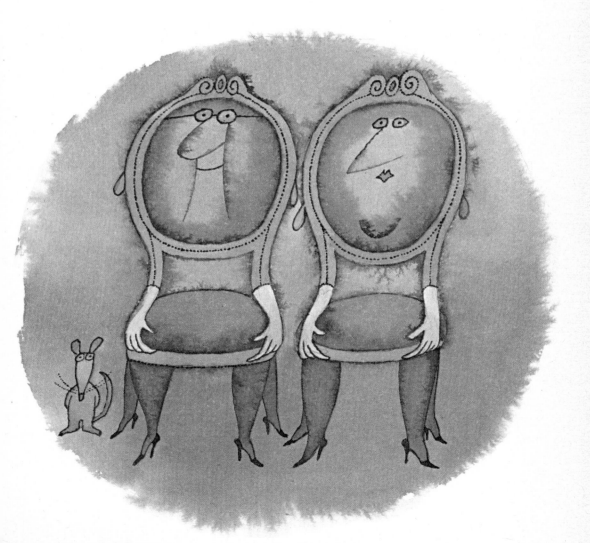

Ottilie and the one thousand, five hundred and eighty inkblots

Writing is really quite easy. You take a blue or green or red fountain-pen, you fill it with blue or green or red ink, and you begin to write. You can write anything: maths homework, New Year's greetings, or anything you want to say. You can write lots of things, because the ink in the fountain-pen lasts a long time – perhaps even up to four days.

But once there was a little girl called Ottilie, who had to fill her pen six times during an afternoon. Every day she bought a bottle of ink, and the woman at the stationer's was at her wit's end, because she couldn't keep up with the demand for all those bottles of ink. She was so amazed that she shook her head and asked: 'Just what *are* you doing with all that ink, my girl? Have you got *so* much to write?'

'I don't know,' replied Ottilie. You see, she was shy and she didn't talk much. But she was also ashamed to explain what was really the matter with her writing. She was ashamed to admit that her writing was dreadful. She knew a lot of things, she could even play carols on her violin, but she couldn't write at all. Just listen to her story.

When the children at school had to write the word 'sparrow', they wrote 'sparrow' and that was it. But with

Ottilie this would never do. Around the sparrow she would make twenty-two blots – seven big ones, four smaller ones, and eleven tiny ones – so that the sparrow was almost drowned in the blots: you see, he was only written down on paper and he couldn't fly away.

But even those twenty-two blots in her exercise-book weren't enough for Ottilie. She made another fifteen on the desk, eight on her skirt, six on her pullover, nine on her stockings, two on her shoes, and four on the ribbon in her hair. She made five on her nose, seven on her forehead, and a huge one on her chin. That made seventy-nine blots in all. Just imagine what it looked like when she was supposed to write an essay at home on half a page, where you can fit in about twenty words. And twenty words multiplied by seventy-nine blots makes one thousand, five hundred and eighty blots. So it's no wonder that the bottle of ink disappeared in no time.

Her dad would spend all evening cleaning the exercise-book with Fado, so that the teacher would be able to find the homework among all those blots. Mum washed the table-cloth, Ottilie's stockings, and her hair-ribbon, she bathed Ottilie, and she grumbled: 'In the morning I'll have to dash again to the cleaner's with your pullover and your skirt. Why do you do this to me, Ottilie? Can't you write carefully? Who do you take after? Your grandpa didn't make blots, and your dad didn't either. When are you going to stop it once and for all?'

Ottilie just shrugged her shoulders. 'I can't help it,' she said. 'It's my pen's fault.'

'Be quiet!' said Dad. 'I've had enough of your excuses. If you make another blot tomorrow, you won't leave the house, just remember that!'

'But tomorrow is the Christmas party,' shouted Mum from the bathroom, 'and Ottilie is going to play carols on her violin. We promised we'd go and listen, and Aunt Sophie is coming too.'

Dad went into the bathroom. 'Christmas party or no Christmas party,' he said, 'if she makes another blot she won't go anywhere, and that's the end of it!'

In the morning Ottilie wanted to look nice for the party, so she put on a white jumper, a green skirt, and white stockings. She took her satchel and her violin, went to school, and sat down at her desk. Then she waited to be told what she should write.

'Children,' said the teacher, 'today we're going to write a dictation piece. Get your exercise-books and your pens ready. And you, Ottilie, will have to write carefully so that you don't just make blots. You know that we have our Christmas party this afternoon.'

She began to dictate: 'The geese cackled, the dogs barked, and the cats miaowed.' She dictated and dictated, while Ottilie thought to herself: 'Christmas party or no Christmas party, if I make any blots I shan't have to play the violin. Anyway, I'd be scared to play in front of so many people.'

So she wrote and wrote, and around those geese she made thirty-eight blots, around the dogs she made eighty-four, and around the cats as many as two hundred and twenty-five. She made three hundred and fifty on her desk, five hundred and eighty on her jumper, sixty-two on her skirt, fifty-seven on her stockings, and three hundred and fifty-five on her mouth – altogether one thousand, five hundred and eighty blots. The bottle of ink had disappeared in no time, and Ottilie put up her hand. 'Please,

Miss,' she said, 'I've got nothing to write with.'

The teacher looked at her and got a shock – there was a proper puddle on the desk, and ink all over Ottilie. Ink wherever you looked. Her jumper looked like a spotted white rabbit, her skirt looked like a spotted green rabbit and her mouth and hands were completely covered with ink. It really was an awful sight.

The teacher clapped her hands to her head. 'Ottilie,' she said, 'what will you look like at the party? What are the dads and mums going to say? I'd rather you didn't play the violin at all, but unfortunately it's the Christmas party and we just can't leave out the carols. You must go home and change.'

But Ottilie said: 'Please, Miss, my dad won't let me go out anyway, he said if I made another blot I'd have to stay at home, and that's the end of it.'

The teacher wondered what to do. She wondered and wondered – then at last she hit on an idea.

'I've got it!' she said, tapping her forehead. 'I'll rinse you in Fado. You'll be dry long before the party begins.' And during break she hurried to the stationer's to buy a whole case of Fado.

The woman at the stationer's just shook her head. 'Why do you need so much Fado?' she asked. 'Where am I going to get all that Fado from? A little girl has already bought up all the ink, and now you want all the Fado. I'd like to know what's going on.'

But the teacher had no time to explain. She hurried back to school, went into the caretaker's flat, and filled the bath with Fado. Then she soaked Ottilie in it from head to toe, soaking her so thoroughly that the blots faded away one after another. But as the blots faded away, Ottilie

12

faded away with them, and before you could say Jack Robinson the bath was empty.

'Come on, Ottilie,' said the teacher, for she thought that Ottilie had just gone somewhere. But Ottilie replied: 'I'm here, Miss, I'm still sitting in the bath.'

The teacher turned as pale as the tiles in the bathroom. 'That's a nice mess,' she said. 'I've Fado'd you so much that you've completely faded away. What will the mums and dads say, and what will become of the Christmas party?'

Ottilie picked up a mirror, and it seemed to the teacher as if the mirror was hanging in mid-air. 'Please, Miss,' she said, 'you're right, I'm completely invisible. But I don't mind that very much – I think I'm going to have a lot of fun like this!'

She had hardly spoken when the bell began to ring. Ottilie ran to her classroom and sat down at her desk, and a moment later the maths teacher came in.

'Today we'll revise multiplication tables,' he said, and he began to ask: 'What is three times five, and what is four times nine?'

'Why should I sit at my desk,' thought Ottilie, 'if nobody can see me anyway?' And she walked quietly round the classroom, and went up to the platform and peeped into the teacher's notebook where he entered the marks. Then she sat down on the teacher's table beside the register, swinging her legs and thinking: 'I wonder if the teacher is going to call me at all?'

When it was Ottilie's turn, the teacher said: 'I see that Ottilie is absent today. I meant to test her and ask her how much seven times eight is.'

Ottilie quickly returned to her desk and said: 'Please,

13

sir, I'm not absent. I'm just invisible. My teacher Fado'd me and I faded away completely.'

The maths teacher raised his eyebrows and said: 'Well, that's different. I thought you were absent,' and he asked her how much seven times eight was, and eight times six.

Ottilie looked in the maths book under her desk and then she answered: 'Please, sir, seven times eight is fifty-six and eight times six is forty-eight.'

'That's right, Ottilie,' said the teacher, 'quite right. Even though I can't see *you* at all, I can see that you're good at maths.' And he gave her full marks.

Ottilie was delighted. 'It's marvellous,' she thought, 'when you're invisible. I'll have nothing but full marks at the end of the year, and without having to learn anything at all!' She was even looking forward to the Christmas party, because she wasn't afraid any more about playing in front of so many people.

In fact, that afternoon Ottilie didn't feel any stage-fright at all. The teacher stepped on to the platform and said to the audience: 'Now our pupil Ottilie will play carols for us on her violin,' and without a trace of nerves Ottilie began to play.

But – you can imagine – instead of listening, the mums and dads whispered: 'What does it all mean? Where *is* Ottilie?' For on the platform the violin was performing as if by itself, the bow was moving to and fro over the strings, while the teacher stood quite unperturbed by the music stand, turning the pages. 'What's all this?' shouted the audience. 'What nonsense!'

The only one who didn't was Aunt Sophie, who was so short-sighted that she could hardly see a thing. She nudged the people sitting next to her and said: 'Do listen

how beautifully Ottilie is playing!'

But Ottilie's mum and dad stood up and went straight to the platform, and said to the teacher: 'That isn't Ottilie! We know Ottilie – we're her parents, after all. There's more to Ottilie than that! She's got hair-ribbons, ears, a neck, and white stockings!'

The teacher realized there was no alternative – she had to admit the truth. 'I'm afraid this *is* your daughter Ottilie,' she said, 'it's just that the poor thing is invisible now. I soaked her in Fado because she was covered with inkblots, and she faded clean away. I really am very sorry indeed,' she said, bursting into tears.

Dad just shook his head. 'So that's the last we've seen of Ottilie,' he said. 'Fado needs to be handled with great care.'

Mum began to wail: 'Oh, my poor little pet, so you're invisible now. Never again shall I wipe the ink from your nose, never again shall I wash you with soap in the bath and take your jumpers and skirts to the cleaners, boo-hoo-hoo!'

Aunt Sophie didn't understand what had happened. 'What a tragedy,' she said through her tears, 'what a tragedy! She must have broken a string or something, and now she can't play the carols!'

But the mums and dads in the hall began to get impatient, and shouted: 'This is a peculiar programme! There ought to have been a choral recital!' And on the platform three people were chanting, all out of tune: '*This isn't a merry Christmas!*'

Mum and Dad and Aunt Sophie decided to leave. They collected their coats from the cloakroom and went home. But Ottilie packed up her violin and walked along with them too, and on the way home she said to them: 'I'm surprised that you're so sad, because it really is marvellous when you're invisible.'

Dad stopped. 'You unfortunate child,' he said. 'You won't ever get anywhere in your life. You can't even be a traffic warden.'

But Ottilie replied: 'I can't be a traffic warden, but I could be a detective in a self-service store.'

Dad said no more.

When they got home, Mum said: 'Now we could go and look at the presents, don't you think?' And they all got up and followed Dad, who lit the candles on the tree and began to hand out the parcels.

Ottilie had three small parcels in front of her. When she unwrapped them, she found in each parcel a brand new fountain-pen, the first red, the second green, and the third blue.

'Those are for you, Ottilie,' said Dad, 'so that you don't make blots any more. You always blamed everything on your pen.'

'Yes, you can try them out at once,' said Mum. 'Send New Year's greetings to Uncle Otto, Aunt Annie and Aunt Clotilda.'

She gave Ottilie three New Year's cards, and Ottilie sat down and wrote: 'Dear Uncle', and as she wrote 'Dear Uncle', she made four hundred and twenty blots around the uncle, five hundred and sixty-six on the table-cloth, and six hundred and ninety-four on her mouth, her hands, and her feet. That made one thousand, five hundred and eighty blots in all.

'Look Dad,' shouted Mum, 'Ottilie's beginning to be visible again! The blots are staying on her!' And Dad said: 'Carry on writing, Ottilie, carry on! Don't let anything put you off!'

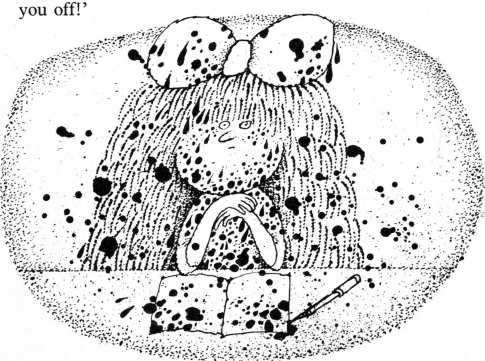

And Ottilie carried on writing, and before she'd finished her greetings cards to her uncle and both aunts she was blue all over with blots, so that she was quite visible again.

Dad gave a sigh of relief. 'Now we've got her back again,' he said, 'our Ottilie.' And Mum and Aunt Sophie said: 'Thank God, now we're rid of this worry.'

Then they all attacked their Christmas dinner. But during the meal, Aunt Sophie – who was very short-sighted indeed – pricked Ottilie with her fork, because she mistook her for the turkey.

Ottilie was furiously cross. 'What a silly girl I am!' she said to herself. 'If I'd taken care not to make any blots I might have stayed invisible, and I might have had lots of fun.'

Hump goes on holiday

The camel hasn't got an easy life –
don't get the idea he has.
No: he carries crates and big boxes of all sorts,
full of bananas and oranges,
and he carries them from morning till night.
And when the day's work is done
he goes and buys himself some chewing-gum,
and he chews.
Why shouldn't he?
It's the only pleasure he has,
and it's a pleasure that costs only a few pennies.
But not all camels are like that.
There was one called Hump
who decided not to spend his money on chewing-gum;
he preferred to save up for a holiday.
On the crates and boxes he carried all day long
he would read strange names of foreign countries and
    cities,
and he said to himself:
'Why shouldn't I go and see what they look like?
Nothing ever happens here –
a few camels chewing gum, that's all.'

20

So he bought a plane ticket and a camera,
and off he went.
But you couldn't say he was exactly *thrilled* with what he
      saw.
Just imagine!
He walked into a foreign restaurant, and
what did he see?
Everybody just sitting there – *chewing!*
Hump was quite disgusted,
and he said to himself:
'What a chump I am!
Is this what I saved up for?
Is this why I gave up my only pleasure?'
So he went straight home
and bought himself some chewing-gum,
just like all the other camels.

Julie and the roast turkey

There are people who seriously believe that knowing about plants isn't very important; they think that maths and grammar are far more useful. But they are wrong there. People who don't know anything about plants may find they have to pay dearly for it. Let's take for instance a *carnivorous* plant – a plant that eats flesh. A lot of people – butchers, salesgirls in delicatessen shops, even policemen – don't know what a carnivorous plant looks like or what it feeds on, but they don't realize how much trouble their ignorance may cause them.

I'll give you an example.

There was once a school where they had a carnivorous plant called Julie in the biology cabinet. She felt quite at home, and in all the years she spent there she had learned a good many things. She knew something about spelling and reading, and about gymnastics and needlework too, so that she was able to run reasonably well, to climb, to crochet, and other things like that. She was looked after by the school caretaker, who lived at the school by himself. Sometimes he took her with him into his flat, and in the afternoons he used to take her for walks on the outskirts of the town. In the evening Julie would mend his socks, and

22

catch flies – you see, a carnivorous plant feeds on live flies.

In summer getting food was easy, because at that time of the year there were plenty of flies. It was worse between autumn and spring, when flies are scarce. But the school caretaker was a kind old man. He caught flies wherever he could, and sometimes he bought a few dried ones in the shop where goldfish were sold. Of course, you know that isn't the same; you can't beat fresh flies. But Julie was sensible and easy to please, and she never complained.

However, one day, just before the Easter holidays, the school caretaker fell ill with measles and had to go to hospital. Everybody at school, including the headmaster, thought hard what to do about Julie, for they were all fond of her.

In the end a little boy called Clifford put up his hand and said he would take Julie home for the holidays. And because Clifford got top marks in biology, and because he knew what a carnivorous plant feeds on, the headmaster said: 'Why not? If he wants to look after her, let him. It's very decent of him to offer.' And so Clifford took Julie home with him.

Clifford's mum was quite beside herself with joy. 'What an exquisite flower!' she cried. 'What colours! My goodness, we've got a visitor for the holidays.' But she didn't know what to give Julie to eat. She offered her ham, sirloin of beef cooked with cream, and goodness knows what else besides.

Clifford lifted up his hands in horror, crying: 'Mum, you can't do that! A carnivorous plant feeds mostly on flies.'

But Mum wouldn't hear of that. 'I'm not going to give her ordinary flies,' she said. 'After all, it's holiday time.'

23

So she offered Julie some roast turkey instead.

And Julie was quite delighted, because she had never eaten anything like it before. She enjoyed the turkey very much and she had no less than eighteen helpings – in fact, she finished off the turkey all by herself. She looked splendid – her stem was like a rolled-up carpet. Mum was pleased about it, and she said: 'Eat it up, eat it up, my dear! I'm so glad you like it.'

But, as you well know, this sort of thing is bound to lead to trouble. When the caretaker came home from hospital he offered Julie three dried flies, but she would not touch the food. She just tore a leaf from her stem and wrote on it: *You can keep your flys. I want turkey. Julie.*

The school caretaker was too surprised to utter a single word. He took the leaf to the headmaster's study.

'What a to-do!' he said. 'Just read this – I don't know what we're going to do about it.'

The headmaster was a sensible man. He just shrugged his shoulders and said: 'Well, for a start, she's made a spelling mistake. Anyway, this is nonsense. There isn't any turkey, and if she doesn't want flies she must go without.'

But it wasn't as easy as that. The following day the caretaker caught some big, fresh bluebottles at the butcher's, but Julie wouldn't even touch them.

Things went on like this for about three days, and then the caretaker took himself off again to the headmaster's study.

'It's no good,' he said. 'She won't eat. What will happen if she dies of hunger? That would be a pity, wouldn't it?'

'Well, yes, that would be a great pity, certainly,' the headmaster agreed. 'But we can't give her turkey. Where would that get us? I'll tell you what you can do – buy her a cheap hot dog, and let's see what happens.'

So the caretaker went out and bought a hot dog. He added a little mustard, and then took it to the biology room on a plate. But Julie was nowhere to be seen. She had disappeared. All that remained of her was a leaf on which she had written: *If you won't giv me turkey, I'm leaving. Julie.*

'What a to-do!' thought the caretaker. He put on his old hat, ran out into the street, and called: 'Julie, Julie! Come back, come back, Julie!' and more words to that effect.

Meanwhile Julie was loitering about the town, looking in shop windows that were full of salami, ham, lobsters, and pheasants. As she stared at all those goodies, her mouth was watering and her stomach was rumbling. All of

a sudden, she saw in the shop window a roast turkey set out on a silver dish and decorated with green lettuce, red tomatoes, and yellow lemons.

Julie couldn't resist the temptation any longer. She went in the shop, and wrote on a leaf: *Some turkey, please, but quikly.*

The shop assistant read the note, and thought: 'This is incredible – a big plant like that, and she doesn't know there's a "c" in "quickly",' but anyway she wrapped up the turkey and gave it to Julie, saying: 'That'll be four pounds twenty pence, please.'

But Julie didn't listen. She unwrapped the turkey and began to eat. She had her mouth full when the shop assistant cried: 'You can't do that! You haven't paid yet and you're already stuffing yourself. That isn't polite –

haven't you got any manners? I don't know what flowers are coming to these days!'

In the end the shop assistant called a policeman. He took the turkey from Julie and led her to a florist's shop. 'Flowers belong with a florist,' he said to the florist. 'Will you keep her here, please? She's been causing a disturbance in the town.'

And that was how, before she knew what was happening to her, Julie came to be put into a vase.

But her luck was in. Into the shop came a man who was just about to get married and was looking for an out-of-the-ordinary bouquet for his bride. So he bought Julie. She was wrapped up in tissue paper, and he took her home and gave her to his bride. The wedding guests were delighted. A lady with a pearl necklace said: 'Oh, what a gorgeous flower! Just right for an occasion like this.'

After the wedding ceremony they all came back to the house and went into a large room where there was a long table with a white table-cloth. The bridegroom took his place with his bride at the head of the table. In front of each guest was a little plate of ham to start the meal.

The bride was holding Julie in her lap. She listened to a man with a white beard who was making a long speech. From time to time everybody clapped.

Julie could stand it no longer. She started to nibble at the ham. But she managed only a few bites before the bride called to a waiter and said: 'Will you please take this flower somewhere cool? It keeps drooping on to my plate.'

And so it happened that Julie found herself in a small, cold room with lots of shelves filled with cakes, salads, pies, and salami, as well as duck, pheasant, and roast turkey.

27

All this set Julie's head spinning. She took off the tissue paper so that it wouldn't be in her way, and she began to eat. She heard the clink of glasses in the large room, but she paid no attention to it. She kept eating, on and on, and when she had polished everything off she wiped her mouth with the tissue paper, and settled down for a nap.

But she didn't get the chance, because the door opened and there was a loud scream – it was the lady with the pearl necklace, shouting: 'Where's the food? Somebody has eaten all the food! Oh, oh, oh!'

All of a sudden the small room was crowded with people wearing dark suits, all of them shaking with cold and anger, all of them looking for the ham and the pies and the turkeys.

Julie tried to reach the door without anyone noticing, but she was unlucky – she knocked over an empty dish. Now things really looked nasty for her. Everyone was running after her, chasing her from one room to the next, falling over chairs and smashing plates. It was a real shambles.

It was lucky for Julie that she could climb, so she was able to drop from the window into the street. From there she ran to the park, stepped on to the lawn and behaved so quietly that you might have thought she was a daisy.

From that day on, strange things began to happen in the town. All sorts of titbits disappeared from larders, kitchens, shops, and restaurants. Every day the newspapers were full of reports about how many sandwiches had disappeared, how many sausages, and – in particular – how many roast turkeys. People read the papers and they were furious about it – and terribly angry with Julie.

Only the children were keeping their fingers crossed for her. They preferred chocolate to pheasants and turkeys, and they said to each other: 'It's fun, isn't it, what Julie is getting up to.' But they whispered it so that they wouldn't be heard by the grown-ups, who were all wishing Julie could be caught.

But who was going to find Julie and catch her – you tell me? Not many people learn about carnivorous plants at school; not many know what such a plant looks like. The cooks, the shop assistants, even the policemen – none of them knew.

So, to be on the safe side, people began to be suspicious of every flower. They refused to keep flowers at home, and outside they picked all the primroses, tulips, and thyme, so that soon, as well as having nothing good to eat, the town was left without any flowers. It wasn't a pleasant sight.

Then someone had the idea that it would be best if they all did a bit of boning-up about plants. Suddenly the school was crowded with people – mums and dads – sitting on small benches, listening, and taking notes. They wrote down what carnations, anemones, and flesh-eating plants looked like.

Next morning when they had boned up their school-notes, they all went out to look for Julie. They looked for her all over the gardens and the parks, but they still couldn't find her.

In the end Julie *was* found – though not by a policeman, or a cook, or a shop assistant. It was the school caretaker, when he went out for his afternoon stroll. Suddenly he heard someone crying – and there sat Julie, reading a newspaper and trembling with fear.

'Julie,' said the old caretaker, 'do you see now where these things lead to? I think you needed this lesson.'

Julie tore a leaf off and wrote: *I am very sory. Julie.*

'Well, you may be sorry now,' said the caretaker. 'But you ought to have thought of the consequences before. People will put up with a lot of things, but you mustn't take their turkeys. When you take their turkeys, then it's a serious matter for them. If you promise to eat flies again and not to give any more trouble, I'll take you back to the school with me, and I won't tell a soul about it.'

So Julie wrote on another leaf, promising to eat flies again. Then the caretaker took off his old hat and put it on her head. As it was already getting dark, everybody thought that he and Julie were two caretakers out for a walk on the streets.

And that was how Julie returned to the biology cabinet at school. She ate flies again, even dried ones, and not a living soul found out she was back, for not many people take an interest in the biology cabinet. Only the head-master knew all about it – and the children, of course. But they kept it to themselves.

How the hedgehogs spent winter

Winter evenings are long and boring,
in the winter there aren't many interesting things to do.
You certainly can't just sleep all the time –
but for a hedgehog, what else is there to do in winter?
What is there for a whole family of hedgehogs to do?
There they lie, just gazing at the ceiling.
They've run out of things to talk about.
It's enough to drive anybody crazy,
the winter drags on such an awful long time,
and they can't go on taking sleeping-pills all the while.
Well, one day this family decided
they'd buy a gramophone
and a record with summer sounds,
such as frogs croaking and things like that.
So they started to save up to buy the gramophone.
They saved up all spring, summer, and autumn,
and then they went out and bought a second-hand
        gramophone
and a record with summer sounds such as frogs croaking.
But – oh dear – when the time came to pay,
they found they had no money left to buy needles.
That was a blow,

you can imagine,
because a gramophone without needles is no use at all.
The hedgehogs were very upset about it,
and they went home in a bad mood.
'We've got a gramophone now,' they said to one another,
'but we'll have to save for another year to buy some
    needles.'
But when they got home, suddenly
the smallest hedgehog started to dance all round the bed-
    room.
The other hedgehogs thought he'd gone crazy,
but the smallest one cried:
'Why should we *buy* needles?
After all, we are hedgehogs, aren't we –
we've got enough needles to last us for fifty years!'
And the hedgehogs looked at one another and started to
    laugh,
and the gramophone started to play,
and it kept playing right through till spring.

Jonah and the whale and the cod-liver oil

There was once a little boy called Jonah, who wanted to be a policeman on traffic duty. But policemen on traffic duty must be very tough so that they don't suffer from the bitter cold in winter, and Jonah was such a delicate little thing – partly because he wouldn't eat fish.

When he scratched his thumb and blew on it to soothe it, he coughed so much that Dad had to run to the telephone and dial 12345, and Doctor Dale came and gave Jonah some drops.

Or, when Jonah looked at a picture-book and turned the pages a little too fast, the draught gave him such a cold that Dad had to run to the telephone and dial 12345, and Doctor Dale came and gave Jonah some powder.

Now one day, just as Jonah was going out with Mum and Dad to see Granny, Aunt Clotilda arrived and brought Jonah some peppermints as a going-away present. Of course, this was a silly thing to do and Aunt Clotilda ought to have had more sense. She ought to have bought a different kind of sweets – jelly babies, for example – but she was thinking of goodness knows what, and so she bought peppermints and gave them to Jonah.

Well, poor little Jonah swallowed one of the

peppermints. As he swallowed, the peppermint scorched his mouth, nearly lifting the roof off it, and it made his ears buzz too; and when he opened his mouth, all the newspapers and old cinema tickets flew all over the place, the table-cloth was fluttering, and Aunt Clotilda and Mum had to hold down their skirts.

It's no laughing matter, having such a gale blowing down your throat, and Jonah of course fell ill with a sore throat. That's even worse than having a cold or a cough, so Dad ran to the telephone faster than usual. He meant to dial 12345 but, because he was thinking that it would be a long time before they could go to Granny's, he dialled 12346 instead. When the doorbell rang a few minutes later, it wasn't Doctor Dale who had come but Mister Whale.

'What can I do for you?' asked Dad.

'You rang me up,' said Mister Whale. 'My number is 12346.'

'That's a mistake,' said Dad, 'I must have dialled the wrong number. I called Doctor Dale, because Jonah has a sore throat.'

'That's all right,' said Mister Whale, 'as it happens, I do know a thing or two about medicine,' and he went straight into the room.

'Good day, Jonah,' said Mister Whale. 'Open your mouth and say *ah* so that I can see what's the matter with you.'

Jonah said *ah*, and Mister Whale looked at his throat and said: 'It's flu. You'll have to gargle thoroughly.'

But Aunt Clotilda wasn't satisfied. She took Dad into the hall and said: 'We can't have Jonah treated by any old whale. What if he doesn't know anything about flu?'

'She's right,' thought Dad, 'there might be nasty complications.' So he went back in the room and asked: 'How can you tell that it's flu? After all, you aren't a doctor, you're just an ordinary whale.'

'And how can you tell that I don't know what I'm talking about,' asked Mister Whale, 'seeing as you're just an ordinary dad? As it happens, I do know what I'm talking about, because when I was small, I was a weak little thing and had flu myself from time to time. These days, of course, I don't know what it means to be ill. That's because I've grown tough in the Arctic Sea and I've been eating plenty of fish and cod-liver oil. Just look at me now! You see? I'm thirty-nine metres long. Jonah must gargle, and then we'll see.'

'Hm,' said Dad, 'perhaps you're right. Jonah must gargle.'

The trouble with Jonah was that he didn't know how to gargle. Mister Whale wanted to show him how to do it, but he had rather a large mouth. So he tried to gargle with the soap and the towel, the telephone and the little bed, but he couldn't manage it. Instead, he swallowed the lot, even the cooker and the saucepan and the radio, and the book of fairy-tales as well. In the end, he managed to gargle and so did Jonah, and they gargled together until Jonah was well again.

'Jonah is well again,' said Mum and Dad and Aunt Clotilda to Mister Whale. 'Thank you very much indeed. You can go home now, we're off to Granny's.'

'Hang on, hang on!' said Mister Whale. 'You may *think* that Jonah's well, but he's not tough enough yet, because he doesn't eat fish or cod-liver oil.'

'Hm,' said Dad, 'perhaps you're right. Jonah must be toughened up. If you can spare the time, stop here with him. We're going to stay with Granny, and when Jonah is tougher you can join us there. Cheerio, then.'

'Cheerio,' said Mister Whale. And he poured cold water into the bowl and called Jonah.

'Jonah, we're going to toughen up. Wash your neck properly with the sponge, and your ears, and all the rest too.'

'Brrr!' said Jonah to himself. 'This water's like ice. I'm not going to wash myself in that!' And he took the sponge, and mopped up all the water in the bowl with it.

'I can't wash myself,' he said to Mister Whale. 'The bowl's quite empty.'

'That's strange,' thought Mister Whale. 'Where could all the water have gone to?' And he poured fresh water into the bowl.

38

Jonah took the sponge, mopped up all the water with it, and said: 'Look, I can't wash myself, because there's no water.'

'Am I going mad?' thought Mister Whale. 'How is it that the water keeps disappearing?' And he poured water into the bowl once more.

And once more Jonah took the sponge, and once more he mopped up all the water in the bowl with it. By now the sponge was getting heavy, because there was as much water in it as there is in a pond.

'Where is all that water going to?' said Mister Whale to himself. And he poured water into the bowl again and again. And this went on until Mister Whale was quite worn out.

'I must have a rest now,' he said to Jonah. 'Let's leave it for the time being.' And he sat down in the chair, where the sponge lay full of water.

In a second the whole place was flooded, in a second there was a sea of water all around them, and in the sea swam Mister Whale, his mouth wide open in astonishment, and in his mouth sat Jonah, shouting: 'All aboard!'

'That's done it,' said Mister Whale. 'Now we're really swimming in an arctic sea. Come inside so that you don't catch cold. You aren't toughened up yet.' He shut his mouth, and Jonah was inside him.

Fortunately, Jonah didn't get on so badly inside Mister Whale. In his stomach he found all sorts of things – a bed, a radio, a fairy-tale book, soap, and a towel – so that he felt quite at home. He switched on a torch, lay down on the bed, and read fairy-tales.

As he was reading, the telephone rang. It was Mister Whale, who asked: 'Aren't you hungry? There's some fish and cod-liver oil in the fridge. Help yourself!'

'No thanks,' said Jonah, 'I don't fancy eating that.'

'All right,' said Mister Whale, 'just help yourself when you're hungry. Go to sleep now, and in the morning I'll teach you how to swim.'

True enough, the next morning the whale opened his mouth and sank to the bottom, and soon he was filled with water. 'Brrr!' cried Jonah. 'The water's cold!'

So he dried himself with the towel and, to get warm, he did some exercises to the music on the radio. And, because he was hungry, he ate some fish and cod-liver oil. After a few days he even liked it, and he had got used to the cold water. In fact, he even went to have a shower upstairs, on Mister Whale's head.

And so he became a quite different little fellow: he'd grown by a head and he weighed twice as much as before, he wasn't worried by even the coldest wind, and because

he was eating fish his bones were like the phosphor which shines in the sea.

'Do you know what, Jonah?' said Mister Whale one day. 'We're going to swim to your Granny's. I think you're ready for it now.'

So they swam to Granny's house. And when they arrived, everybody was amazed to see them.

'That can't be Jonah, our delicate little boy,' said Granny and Mum and Dad and Aunt Clotilda.

'It is me!' said Jonah, 'I'm not a delicate little boy any more.'

'I'd like to give you some more of my peppermints for a welcome-home present,' said Aunt Clotilda, 'but you know what happened last time.'

'Huh!' said Jonah, and gobbled up five bags of peppermints at one go. And when he opened his mouth, Aunt Clotilda was flying in the air for a fortnight!

Jonah said goodbye to Mister Whale and thanked him, and he did become a policeman on traffic duty. He never suffered from the cold, not even during the coldest of frosts, and at night he shone like a neon sign, so that all the drivers were very grateful to him, especially when it was foggy. They were very fond of him, they knew him by name, and they'd say:

'You're a shiner, Jonah!'

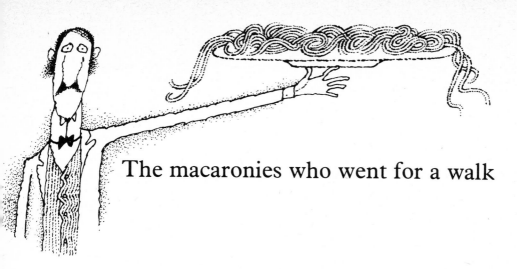

The macaronies who went for a walk

To live in a box and never see a thing – that must be an awful bore. There they were, lying in a box in the larder, bored stiff: about a hundred and twenty sticks of macaroni. They were Italian macaronies, so they spoke to each other in Italian.

'What a bore,' they said, 'what a bore.'

'It's so boring,' said one macaroni, 'we're bored to the teeth – in fact, we could end up eating one another.'

'Well, we can't eat one another raw,' said macaroni number three. 'But why don't we go somewhere? The world is so interesting, after all. It has roundabouts and swings and all sorts of concerts, fancy restaurants, zoos, and goodness knows what else.'

'All right,' said macaroni number nine, 'but will they let us go? People will see us and they'll say: "Ah! macaronies!" and they'll grab hold of us, and that'll be the end of our walk.'

'We mustn't be recognized,' said macaroni number thirty-seven, 'so let's wear hats and raincoats.'

So they put on hats and raincoats and off they went. They walked the streets, all hundred and twenty of them, and people said: 'Look! Some sort of guided tour.'

From time to time the macaronies stopped people who were passing by and asked in Italian: 'Excuse us, do you know any interesting sights around here?'

'The trouble is,' people said, 'we don't know any Italian, but if you want to see something interesting, we've got a roundabout and swings, all sorts of concerts, a fancy restaurant and a zoo, and goodness knows what else.'

'Well, perhaps we'll try the roundabout and the swings first, and then a concert and the zoo,' said the macaronies.

'Well, in that case you go such and such a way,' people said, and the macaronies walked on and visited the roundabout and swings, and a concert, and the zoo. It was all very interesting, but in the end the macaronies felt cold, their feet were frozen, and they said to one another:

'It was all very interesting. All macaronies ought to see things like that. But now let's go and sit down in a restaurant.'

So they went into a restaurant, sat down quietly, and chatted together in Italian. When the waiter heard them, he said to himself: 'I know how to please them – I'll bring them Italian macaroni. They'll enjoy that!' And that's just what he did – he brought them macaroni.

As you can imagine, it was a pleasant surprise for the macaronies – the ones sitting at the table as well as the ones lying on the plates – and they all said at once: 'What a coincidence! What are you doing here?'

'Well,' said the macaronies sitting on the chairs, 'we were bored stiff, so we went for a little walk and, because our feet were hurting us, we called here.'

'Why didn't we think of that before now?' said the macaronies on the plates to one another. 'We might have seen something ourselves.'

45

'It's never too late. We've already seen all sorts of things. But you haven't seen any. Let's change places – you take our hats and raincoats, and we'll lie down on the plates. It's quite simple. Let's get on with it!'

So the macaronies that were lying on the plates jumped down on to the carpet. But the head waiter came running up and said to the ones at the table:

'Excuse me, I don't know any Italian, but what sort of manners have you got? All the macaroni is on the carpet. I thought you knew how to eat macaroni.' And he hurried away to fetch a dustpan and brush.

'Here are the hats and the raincoats,' said the first group of macaronies to the second. 'Get dressed while we get on to the plates.' And they climbed on to the plates, dipped their feet in the hot sauce, and felt fine.

When the head waiter arrived with the dustpan and brush, he saw that there were no macaronies on the carpet and that the guests were leaving. He was very surprised.

'Why are you leaving?' he wanted to know. 'Didn't you like the macaroni?'

'Excuse us,' said the macaronies who were about to leave, 'but how could we eat raw macaroni? Since when is genuine Italian macaroni eaten raw?'

The head waiter looked, and he saw that the macaronies on the plates really were raw. He made his apologies, thinking: 'What a disgrace!'

But the macaronies wearing hats and raincoats smiled and said: 'Never mind, that can easily happen.'

And they waved goodbye to the raw macaronies, and went out to have a look at the swings and the roundabout, and at the whole world that is so very interesting.

Matilda gets a spare head

A head is just a small box full of tiny drawers and compartments where knowledge can be stored, in the same way as handkerchiefs in a chest-of-drawers. When Mum tells us: 'Eat your greens, children, they're good for you,' her words pass through our ears straight into those small compartments, and afterwards if anybody asks us: 'What use are greens?' we look into our heads and answer with a complete sentence. 'Greens,' we say, 'are good for us.'

Of course, we must have order in our heads so that we can find whatever we're looking for, or it would take ages before we could answer any question about greens. That's why it's best to store in our heads only what is important, so that we're not lumbered with useless things. Someone who has his head full of nonsense is bound to get mixed up eventually, and if anybody asks him: 'Do you happen to know how many feet a dog has?' the poor thing will just stand there, gazing around, tapping his forehead, and muttering: 'Well, it's like this, I have it on the tip of my tongue, but I just can't remember.'

But that's not true. People like that carry so many useless things about with them in their heads that in the end there's no room left for important things.

For example, there was once a little girl called Matilda. She looked just like other little girls: there was nothing out of the ordinary about her, except that she wore blue ear-rings. Matilda's head was full of things such as letters, commas, full stops, hyphens, and useless words, as it were – and all this simply because she learned everything by heart. She would learn and learn until she knew all about the subject, including all the letters and commas. Then her mum would give her a chocolate wrapped in silver paper, and say: 'I'm very pleased with you. If you always learn so nicely, you'll be the cleverest girl in the world.'

No wonder that Matilda got nothing but ten out of ten at school – except in gymnastics, that is; you see, you can't learn somersaults from books. But even so, she was top of the school. And when the teacher called her and said: 'Now then, Matilda, stand up straight and tell us something about crocodiles,' even the headmaster stopped outside the door when he was passing by, and listened. Matilda repeated simply everything that was written in the book about crocodiles, including what was written between the brackets.

When Matilda had finished talking about crocodiles, the teacher stroked her head. 'I *am* pleased, Matilda,' she said, 'I can see that you are really working hard at home. And you, children, ought to take Matilda as an example. I must send for the school inspector so that he can hear for himself what a model pupil we have in our class.' And she gave Matilda ten out of ten and a star.

Of course, the other children worked at home too, learning about crocodiles: what they look like, where they live, and what they live on. But when the teacher called their names, they answered rather casually. They said the first thing that came into their heads, but that wasn't good enough. Nobody stopped outside the door to listen to them, and they only rarely got ten out of ten and a star; while Matilda got them every time.

You can imagine, she was rather conceited about her top marks – so conceited, in fact, that she wouldn't talk to some of the other children. When she was in the mood, she would say to them: 'Heh, one day I'll be the cleverest girl in the world, heh!' After school she would run straight home and not go out any more, not even to the playground. She looked a little green in the face, but that didn't worry her. She just sat and sat and learned. She learned by heart the whole of her arithmetic book and her English book, and once – just imagine! – even the whole of the railway timetable and the bus timetable as well, including the additional notes. So she knew all the express train times, all the slow train times, and all the bus times, and where you had to change. Nothing but numbers and hours and minutes.

Mum was full of praise for Matilda. 'You're my good girl,' she said. 'It's very difficult to understand a timetable, it takes ages to find anything. Now it'll be easier for us, and when we go to stay with Aunt Clotilda on Sunday to wish her many happy returns of the day, I'll ask: When does the train leave? and you'll tell me, and that'll be it!' And she stroked Matilda's head and gave her a chocolate wrapped in silver paper. Out of the window went the timetable.

At school, Matilda said to the other children: 'Heh, I know the whole timetable by heart. I know all the express train times, all the slow train times, and all the bus times, and you know nothing, heh!'

The children were about to say: 'You silly thing, why do you learn all that? What's the use of knowing the timetable by heart!' But they didn't get the chance, because the bell was ringing and the teacher came in and began to talk about polar bears.

'Well, children,' she said in the end, 'you'll be good and learn all about polar bears at home, and tomorrow I'll see what you know about them.'

'Right!' thought Matilda. 'I'll learn all about the polar bears in no time, then I'll learn something else by heart – perhaps the telephone directory.' But when she came home, her mum told her: 'It's Friday today, my darling, and on Sunday we're going to visit Aunt Clotilda. I've written down some greetings for you to learn by heart, so that you can wish her many happy returns of the day.'

Matilda sat down and learned the birthday greetings by heart. It was easy. Hardly seven pages, and nothing but 'dear Auntie' and 'dearest Auntie' and 'darling Auntie'. Before you could say Jack Robinson, Matilda knew it all. She was given a chocolate wrapped in silver paper, and she carried on learning.

Next she began to learn about polar bears, but – would you believe it? – hardly had she learned the first sentence when she got stuck. Whatever she did, she couldn't learn any more. She was scared out of her wits. She ran to the kitchen, looking for her mum. 'Mum,' she cried, 'what shall I do? I'm learning about polar bears, but I simply can't remember anything.'

Mum laughed. 'Come on,' she said, 'what are you talking about? You can't remember – a clever girl like you? Just stand up straight as you do at school, and try once more.'

Matilda stood up straight and began: 'On the white plains of the Far North, where no human foot treads – as it were; among the eternal snows and the eternal ice, there live the polar bears, who are all . . .' and that was it!

Mum said: 'Now then, Matilda, go on. You must mention that the bears are all white, do you understand? Of course you do. Now then, repeat once more!'

Once more Matilda began: 'On the white plains of the Far North, where no human foot treads – as it were; among the eternal snows and the eternal ice, there live the polar bears, who are all . . .'

Full stop! Matilda didn't say another word. She simply couldn't go on. Up to now she had always found learning so easy, but now the drawers and compartments of her head were full of express trains and slow trains and buses, and full of numbers and hours and minutes too, and it seemed there really was no more room for anything in the girl's head. Mum threw up her hands in despair, crying: 'Oh my poor Matilda, my poppet, you know the arithmetic book by heart but you can't remember that polar bears are all white!'

Suddenly Mum had an idea. 'Don't cry, Matilda,' she said. 'If you can get spare flints for lighters, spare buttons for winter coats, and spare wheels for cars – why then shouldn't there be spare heads for little girls?' And she rushed off to the department store.

When she came back, she said: 'Look! I've chosen one in green.' And she opened a box and took out a spare head which could be screwed on. It was a head just like the heads that all little girls have, nothing out of the ordinary. It was a simple matter to add blue ear-rings, and then it looked exactly like Matilda. 'You see, Matilda,' said Mum, 'all is well again. You've got a new head now. It's quite empty, and you can learn as much as you like with it.'

Once more Matilda settled down to work. In no time she knew simply everything about polar bears, down to the last letter and the last comma. She said to herself: 'Now I'm going to learn the telephone directory by heart.' And she did – all of it, and that's quite an achievement, because the telephone directory is a big book full of names, and every one of them has a different number. But Matilda managed to learn them all in less than two hours.

'Matilda,' said Mum, 'I'm very pleased with you. It's very complicated to find a number in the telephone directory, it usually takes ages. But from now on things will be much easier. When I need a number I'll just ask you and that'll be it.' And she gave Matilda a chocolate wrapped in silver paper. Out of the window went the telephone directory.

The following morning Matilda said to the children at school: 'Heh, I've got a new head and you've got nothing, heh!' The children wanted to say something but they didn't get the chance, because the bell started ringing.

In came the teacher with the school inspector. 'Children,' said the teacher, 'I was going to examine you to see what you know about polar bears, but let's revise crocodiles instead. Now then, Matilda, perhaps you'll answer. Stand up straight, the inspector is listening to you.'

Matilda stood up straight and opened her mouth, but that was about all she did. She just stared and stared, and didn't utter a single word. The teacher gazed at the ceiling, whispering: 'Now then, Matilda, hurry up!' And the inspector swayed on his toes, clearing his throat now and then. After this had been going on for twenty-four minutes, the teacher said: 'Sit down, Matilda. You've got nought out of ten. That'll teach you! What a disgrace!'

Matilda began to sob bitterly and she got the hiccups. 'Please, Miss,' she complained, 'I don't want nought out of ten. After all, I know simply everything about the crocodiles, but the crocodiles are in my old head. In my new head I've only got polar bears and the telephone directory.'

'We may as well make sure this pupil is telling the truth,' said the inspector. So he asked Matilda to tell him the telephone number of his neighbour, Mrs Zyzzle, and Matilda answered: 'Zyzzle, Zoe, 6374 8596.'

'This is almost unbelievable!' cried the inspector, and

53

the teacher smiled at him, and said: 'Matilda promises that from next Monday she'll bring both her heads to school, the old one and the new one, so we may as well forgive her those crocodiles today.' The inspector agreed, and Matilda was glad everything had turned out in this way.

At home she told her mother: 'I'll have to take the old head along in my satchel as well. Today things almost turned out disastrously for me.' But Mum listened with only one ear to what Matilda was saying, because she was brushing her suit in the hall, combing her hair in the bathroom, painting her finger-nails in the living-room, running to and fro, and calling: 'Matilda, hurry up! We're going to visit your aunt. Wash your neck and your ears and put on your white stockings! There isn't much time. When does the train leave?'

But Matilda didn't know what her mother was talking about, because she had the railway times in the old head which was lying on the kitchen table. Mum began to shout: 'What a waste of time! Am I supposed to change your head now?'

There was no choice: they had no railway timetable at home, so Mum had to screw Matilda's old head on, and when she'd done so, Matilda said: 'Our train leaves in five minutes, and there isn't another one.'

Matilda wanted to put the new head on again, but Mum said: 'Are you crazy, Matilda? It's high time for us to go. You're travelling with your old head, and that's final. We'll be lucky if we make it, even with a taxi. What's the number of the taxi-rank?'

But Matilda didn't know what her mum was talking about, because the telephone directory was in her new head. 'That's the last straw!' cried Mum. 'Am I supposed to screw your new head on again now? We're sure to miss that train.'

But they had no choice: there was no telephone directory at home, so Mum had to change Matilda's heads over, and when she'd done so, Matilda said: 'The number is 8765 4321.'

Mum dialled the number. 'Will you please come to Cauliflower Street right away?' she asked. 'We're in a hurry because we've a train to catch.'

The taxi arrived in no time and they set off at great speed for the station, ignoring all the traffic lights. Suddenly Mum exclaimed: 'Stop! Turn back! Your birthday greetings for Aunt Clotilda are in your old head that's lying on the kitchen table!'

So they set off home again at great speed, ignoring the traffic lights, and they dashed into the kitchen and picked up the head from the table. 'Hurry!' cried Mum. 'Put it in the string bag, we'll change them over in the taxi. No time to do it now.'

Back they ran again and sat down in the taxi, where Mum put Matilda's old head on in place of her new one – not forgetting the blue ear-rings. The taxi-driver thought the two of them were probably crazy, but he said nothing and just drove as fast as he could. But when they arrived outside the railway station they found that the train had already left.

'That's it,' said Mum, 'the train has gone and there isn't another one. What a mess we're in!' They had no reason to hurry now, so they caught a bus home.

On the way, a fat woman with glasses got on, carrying a cabbage in her string bag. She wanted to sit down but there was no empty seat, so the conductor said to Matilda:

'Come on, at least take the lady's bag and hold it for her.'

Matilda frowned: she was holding one string bag already, and now she was supposed to hold another one. But as everybody was looking at her, she put the second bag on her knees too.

The bus went on and on, and Mum began to stare at the cabbage. 'Where did you get that fine big cabbage?' she asked.

'I telephoned the shop in Kangaroo Street,' said the woman in glasses, 'and they said they had just come in.'

On and on went the bus. At last it stopped at Cauliflower Street, and Matilda gave the string bag back to the fat woman. The woman thanked her and said: 'See you again, I hope.'

Matilda and her mum got off and went home, but as they walked into the kitchen, Matilda suddenly cried: 'Mum! Just look what I've got in my string bag!'

Mum looked, and threw up her hands. This wasn't Matilda's bag. It was the fat woman's bag, and in it was the cabbage.

'Matilda,' said Mum, 'you clumsy thing, why aren't you more careful? You can't put a cabbage on your neck! We must find your string bag. I'm going to telephone the lost property office. Tell me the number!'

But Matilda didn't know what her mum was talking about, because the telephone directory was in the head that was in the string bag. So Mum had to go and ask the neighbours for their telephone directory.

But the neighbours said: 'What? You fling your telephone directory out of the window and then you expect us to lend you ours? You must be joking!'

There was no choice: Mum had to go to the phone-box. She searched for coins in her handbag and in her purse, in the drawers, in her mugs, and in her money-box. She took out all the coins she needed and rang up all the lost property offices, but without success.

'What am I going to do now?' she said to herself. 'It's Sunday, the shops are closed, I can't get hold of the new head, and on Monday Matilda needs it at school as well as the old one – or else! I know – I'll ring up all the numbers in the telephone directory. That woman must have a telephone, after all. Sooner or later she'll have to answer the phone.'

So Mum pushed one coin after another into the coin-box, and dialled and dialled; and, as telephone directories are arranged in alphabetical order, she spoke first to Mrs Abbott, then to Mrs Abcott, then to Mrs Abdott. . . . But none of them knew anything about Matilda's head.

Meanwhile, a crowd of people had gathered outside

the phone-box. There were about four hundred of them, all shouting.

'I'm sorry,' said Mum, 'but we've lost a head. There's nothing we can do.' And the people shouted, 'If this goes on much longer, we'll lose our heads too!'

Mum shut the door of the phone-box again, and she called Mrs Allan, and Mrs Alman, and Mrs Alpan. . . .

Matilda waited at home. Evening came, but there was still no trace of her mother. Eventually, at midnight, Matilda yawned and said to herself: 'This is impossible. She must come home any minute now.'

But no – Mum was still pushing coin after coin into the phone-box, and dialling, and she called Mrs Barry, and Mrs Bassey, and Mrs Batty. . . .

Meanwhile outside the phone-box there was a queue of almost nine thousand people.

At home Matilda was sleeping like a log – she'd fallen asleep fully dressed, just as she was, she hadn't even cleaned her teeth. She just slept and slept.

When she opened her eyes it was a quarter to nine. Outside, the sun was shining. In the hall stood Mum.

'Matilda,' said Mum, 'just think how lucky I was! In the end I did find that fat woman after all. She's called Zoe Zyzzle, she's the last in the whole directory. Her number was 6374 8596. She promised to come round at once so that you don't miss school.'

But she had hardly finished speaking when the bell rang. It was Mrs Zyzzle, and she came in wearing her glasses and carrying a string bag, and in the string bag was Matilda's new head.

'Just fancy!' said Mrs Zyzzle. 'We very nearly ate it. You see, I'm very short-sighted, and I thought it was a cabbage. I'm sorry, but I noticed my mistake a little too late, so it was partly boiled – but fortunately nothing's happened, except that it's a bit on the red side now.'

Mum waved her hand. 'Never mind,' she said, 'as a matter of fact, that head looks healthier now than it did before.' She handed the fat woman her string bag, screwed Matilda's new head on her, and said: 'Hurry! You must get to school on time!'

Matilda left home in a hurry. In the street, crowds of people were standing in a queue in front of a phone-box. Matilda ran on as fast as she could and she managed to arrive at school on time, just as the bell was ringing.

The teacher walked into the classroom. 'Children,' she said, 'you had to learn all about polar bears for today. Let's see now what you know about them. Stand up, Matilda. Last time, your performance was poor. I hope you'll deserve full marks today. Stand up straight and begin.'

Matilda stood up straight and began: 'On the white plains of the Far North, where no human foot treads – as it were; among the eternal snows and the eternal ice, there live the polar bears, who are all boiled.'

The teacher said: 'That'll do, Matilda. What nonsense are you talking? Begin once more, and think what you're saying.'

Matilda began once more: 'On the white plains of the Far North, where no human foot treads – as it were; among the eternal snows and the eternal ice, there live the polar bears, who are all boiled.'

'I've had enough of this nonsense,' said the teacher. 'Sit down, Matilda. You've got nought out of ten. Polar bears live on ice, not on the cooker.' And the children laughed, shouting: 'Matilda's crazy!'

60

Matilda sat down looking very cross, because she had been given nought out of ten. 'I did learn all about polar bears by heart, I really did,' she thought, 'and I only said what I've got in my head.'

True, she had said only what she had in her head but, poor thing, everything she had in her head had been partly boiled. There were lots of 'dear boiled aunts', plenty of 'beloved boiled aunts', and a couple of 'dearest boiled aunts' too. In her head she had a whole boiled set of birthday greetings and a complete boiled telephone directory – in short, she had her whole head partly boiled, and if that happens, then even polar bears are boiled! And there is nothing anyone can do about it.

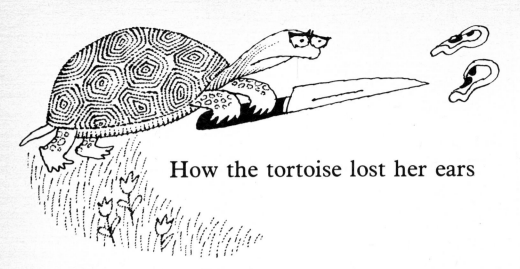

How the tortoise lost her ears

The giraffe has ears, the cat has ears, even the kangaroo has ears; only the tortoise hasn't any. Yet she could have had them, she could have looked like all the other animals. It was all her own fault, because she didn't like the sound of singing. Look what happens if you're grumpy.

The tortoise lived in one room with a bird, and the bird used to sing, the way all birds do when they see spring for the first time. He sang from morning till evening, but the tortoise liked to sleep late. She had plenty of time to sleep, she had time to sleep for a hundred years or longer. She was in no hurry to go anywhere, and there was nothing that interested her at all. She had lived too long already, and the bird got on her nerves.

At first the tortoise thought: 'I can put up with it for a few years. The bird can't sing for ever, and next century I'll have peace again. Lucky for me that I'm a tortoise!' But after seventeen years she got fed up with it all, and so at suppertime she invited a cat who liked eating birds.

The cat came. She was hungry, but she behaved like a perfect lady. 'You've got a nice place here,' she said. 'I'd like a view over the rooftops like this myself.' And the bird sang, the way birds do when they see spring for the seventeenth time. Why shouldn't he? After all, the cat wasn't *his* guest.

Well, the tortoise tried dropping hints to the cat, that she could have the bird for supper if she made a little effort. But, would you believe it – the cat just wasn't in the mood. 'I've eaten too many songbirds already,' she said, 'they're all singing inside my stomach now. Just listen!'

The tortoise was very upset at having to listen to all that singing. It was more than she could stand. 'If you'll excuse me,' she said to the cat, 'I'll go and have a wash – I can't sit down to supper like this.' And she went to the bathroom and cut off both her ears.

Now the tortoise had all the peace she wanted, because she had nothing but silence. She left her ears lying under the wash-basin. 'Ears', she said, 'are strictly for the birds.' But it wasn't the birds who ate them, it was the cat – and the cat didn't feel the least bit offended, because it was a long time since she had had tortoise-ears for supper.

The bird sang and the cat ate, and when the cat had finished she said: 'That was delicious! Well, bye, bye!'

But the tortoise didn't say anything, because she couldn't hear, and the cat thought: 'What a rude tortoise! How can that bird stand living with her!'

The boy who was turned into a cupboard

There are as many children in the world as there are specks of dust. They're all a bit naughty: some slide down the banisters, some suck their fingers, some clink with their knife and fork, some won't eat macaroni, some scribble in their books, some suck everything they can lay their hands on, some forget to say 'how do you do?', some make a mess on the table-cloth, some just won't go to bed. In a word – *all* children are naughty one way or another. And that's why somebody hit on the idea of calling a meeting to discuss what was to be done.

It really was a big meeting. All the dads and all the mums came, some from as far as Africa, some from Australia, and eventually even two grannies from the North Pole, who turned up to watch just out of interest.

'Now then,' said the fat man with glasses who had called the meeting. 'All the mums and all the dads are here, I hope?'

But no! A woman with a green hat put her hand up. 'Excuse me,' she said, 'one dad and one mum are missing.'

'One dad and one mum are missing? Why?' asked the fat man with glasses. 'What is this – Noah's Ark?'

'They're missing because at home they have a little boy called Jolly, and he's the best-behaved little boy in the world. Why should *they* ask for advice?' said the woman with the green hat as she sat down. Then all the mums and dads shouted: 'It isn't possible!'

But the fat man with glasses rang a tiny bell. 'Silence!' he said. 'We can't all talk at the same time. What is this – a mad-house? In any case, the best thing will be to have a look at Jolly, and if he is really the best-behaved little boy in the world we'll let him appear on television, so that the other children can take him as an example.'

And all the mums and dads clapped, because the television idea greatly appealed to them. 'A lot of nonsense is shown on television,' they thought, 'but this programme will serve a good purpose.'

The fat man with glasses took his hat. 'Wait here,' he said. 'Don't go away! We'll go and fetch Jolly. The train leaves in twenty minutes.' He took with him the woman in the green hat, who knew where Jolly lived. They bought some peanuts to eat on the train, and they soon reached the house where Jolly lived.

'Good day,' said the fat man with glasses when Jolly's dad answered the door. 'We've come to have a look at your little boy to see if he really is the best-behaved little boy in the world.'

'Please do,' said Dad. 'At the moment Jolly's in the bathroom, washing his ears for the twelfth time.'

'I beg your pardon, what did you say?' asked the fat man with glasses.

'He's washing his ears for the twelfth time,' repeated Dad. 'Jolly washes his ears eighteen times every day.'

'Aha!' exclaimed the fat man with glasses, and he

wrote something down in his notebook. 'And does he wash his ears of his own free will?'

'Of course,' said Jolly's mum. 'He also goes of his own free will to the dentist for a check-up twice a day.'

'Could we see your little boy?' asked the fat man with glasses. Dad opened the door and called Jolly, who came in with red, perfectly clean ears, and said: 'How do you do? I am Jolly. Very pleased to meet you.'

'Just a minute,' said the fat man with glasses, and he wrote in his notebook: *Jolly says 'Pleased to meet you'*. Then he shook hands with Jolly and asked him several questions, such as: 'What do you do all day, Jolly?' and more questions of that kind.

'If I am not washing my ears or waiting in the dentist's waiting-room,' replied Jolly, 'I sit by the table, taking care not to kick the chairs.'

'That can't be possible,' said the fat man with glasses.

'Excuse me,' objected Dad, 'but Jolly doesn't tell lies. The whole town knows what Jolly's like. The pupils from the primary schools and the nursery schools come to have a look at him on Wednesdays and Fridays – it's compulsory for them. They can all testify to it – Jolly's better-behaved than even a canary or a lamb.'

'What are you saying?' Mum interrupted Dad. 'Jolly's even better-behaved than the furniture. Look at that old kitchen cupboard! It's creaking so badly that we'll have to throw it out, but Jolly never creaks.'

At that moment Jolly cleared his throat. 'If you will permit me to do so,' he said, 'I shall go into the garden with my ball for a while. It is not fitting that I should overhear what is said about me.' With that he left the room. The fat man with glasses and the woman with the

green hat stood open-mouthed, for they had never heard anything like it.

Jolly walked round the garden. From time to time he jumped, and threw his ball up into the air. But – oh, dear! – as the ball came down, it got stuck in a tree.

'What am I to do now?' said Jolly to himself. 'I can't climb up the tree, because only uneducated people, apes, and monkeys climb up trees; but I can't go indoors without my ball either. I wouldn't think of it – losing things is irresponsible, to say the very least.' Jolly just stood there not knowing what to do. He felt like crying, and he sobbed a little under the tree.

Then suddenly he had an idea. What if he climbed quickly up the tree, and down again just as quickly? What if he did it without being seen? All would be well if he got away with it.

So he put a ladder against the tree, climbed up the tree, threw the ball down to the ground, and began to climb down. But the moment he started to get down he saw two people in the garden with saws. They came straight up to the tree he was hiding in, and said to each other: 'This is the cherry-tree for the new kitchen cupboard then, isn't it?' And before Jolly knew what was happening, the saw was moving to and fro.

'If I make a noise now,' thought Jolly, 'the whole town will know that I climb trees like uneducated people, apes, and monkeys, and everybody will say: "This is *not* the best-behaved little boy, definitely not, he is just an ordinary naughty boy."'

Whatever happened, he told himself, he wouldn't make a noise or climb down. And when the tree fell, he held tightly on to it so that he wouldn't fall down from it on to the lawn. And so he was put on the lorry together with the tree, and was taken to the carpenter's.

At the carpenter's it smelled of glue and freshly-cut wood. There was a great deal of noise, but Jolly didn't utter a word, or move an inch. He kept as still as if he was made of wood, which for him was quite natural. And so, naturally, he was made into boards for making kitchen cupboards.

'Nobody will recognize me now I've been turned into boards,' thought Jolly with satisfaction. And indeed everybody praised the beauty and hardness of the wood, a fine new cupboard was made out of him, it was painted and polished, and then it was sent to his mum's and dad's and put in the kitchen.

There in the kitchen stood Mum and Dad – dressed in black and crying. The fat man with glasses shook his head. 'What a tragedy!' he said. 'The best-behaved little boy in the world disappears just as he's about to appear on television. That really is bad luck, don't you think?' But Mum just wiped her nose and kept repeating: 'Jolly, Jolly, we've got a new cupboard that doesn't creak and you, my poor pet, don't know it!'

'Why shouldn't I know about the cupboard,' cried Jolly, 'it's *me*, after all!'

Mum and Dad threw up their hands, and the fat man with glasses and the woman with the green hat threw up their hands. Everybody was throwing up their hands, everybody was astonished, there was no end of questions.

In the end the fat man with glasses said: 'That'll do, you can talk about it later. Right now we must hurry to the meeting.' With the help of the woman with the green hat he wrapped Jolly in wood-shavings, then they bought peanuts for the journey and off they went.

By now the meeting looked like playtime at school: the dads were throwing paper darts, the mums were knitting, and one dad was standing by the door to keep watch. When he saw the fat man with glasses and the woman with the green hat, he shouted: 'Here they come!' And every-body sat down and behaved as if nothing had happened.

The door opened and in came the fat man with glasses and the woman with the green hat, followed by railway porters carrying a big package wrapped in wood-shavings, and a crowd of people from television carrying lamps and a camera. The fat man with glasses announced: 'We man-aged to bring along the best-behaved little boy in the world. Silence, please! As soon as we unpack him, give him a warm welcome, but behave yourselves, please! Remember, the welcome will be televised for all the world to see.'

'Excuse me, why is he wrapped up in wood-shavings?' asked one dad after getting permission to speak.

'So that he wouldn't get knocked about,' said the woman with the green hat. 'That would be a pity, because he is after all the best-behaved little boy in the world.'

'Oh, I see,' said the dad, and sat down. All the parents watched as the railway porters removed the paper and the wood-shavings. It took them some time, but in the end there emerged a big white cupboard.

'This is our Jolly,' said the fat man with glasses. 'Please, mums and dads, give him a hearty welcome.'

But the mums and dads didn't feel like welcoming anybody. They just looked at one another. Eventually one mum put her hand up. 'Excuse me,' she asked, 'is Jolly *inside* the cupboard, or . . . ?'

'No,' answered the woman with the green hat, 'inside there are mugs, pots, wooden spoons, tin saucepans, and a large salad bowl.'

'Oh, I see,' said the mum.

Then there was a deep silence, until the fat man with glasses began to clap his hands and cried: 'Long live Jolly! Long live Jolly!' But nobody joined in the clapping, except for one dad, who was standing in the front row and couldn't hide behind anybody.

'This is no boy, it's a cupboard,' whispered one mum to another, and the other mum whispered back: 'It's obvious it's a cupboard. I know what a cupboard's like, after all. We've had three of them, and they all looked exactly the same.' But the dads were shouting: 'Of course it's a cupboard – we're not blind!'

The fat man with glasses stopped clapping his hands. He got very angry and shouted: 'Why shouldn't he be the best-behaved little boy? We've seen him, haven't we, when he was washing his ears for the twelfth time? What does it matter that he was turned into a cupboard? Just look! Instead of all kinds of silly things in his head he now has lovely mugs, all nicely arranged.' With that he opened the cupboard, and everybody saw that everything in Jolly's head was indeed in perfect order.

'Everything's in order, that's true,' said one mum. 'But if only he could run and jump like other children! He just stands and stares.'

'Hm,' said the fat man with glasses, bending towards Jolly, 'couldn't you perhaps turn a somersault, so that these people can leave you in peace?'

'Yes, of course I could,' answered Jolly, and he made a tiny step forward and bowed. 'If you don't believe that I am a little boy I'll turn a somersault – even though usually only uneducated people, apes, and monkeys turn somersaults.'

And that's what he did – he turned a somersault. But it was a mistake for him to turn a somersault, it was a big mistake, because he rubbed off all his paint, he broke all the mugs and plates, he jumbled up the wooden spoons and knives and forks, and he broke the pots and finally the salad bowl as well. When he stood upright again, he looked dreadful – a scratched, broken mess of a cupboard – and all the mums and dads shouted: 'It's outrageous! Even if he is the best-behaved little boy in the world, we don't want children like him. We prefer our children as they are!' And they all looked for their cloakroom tickets and left in a hurry.

Just imagine it! The whole event was shown on television in all corners of the world. Everywhere, children were sitting around their TV sets, and they pointed to the broken cupboard and laughed, while some of them clinked with their knife and fork, some sucked everything they could lay their hands on, some kicked their chairs, and all of them refused to go to bed.

The naughty frog

With children there's always trouble.
I'll give you just one example:
there was a little frog
whose mum and dad wanted her to be properly dressed,
so they went to a clothes shop to buy
a nice green plastic mac.
But the little one didn't like it,
she wanted a blue coat with goodness knows what kind of
    fastenings.
But Dad said: 'Be sensible,
all frogs wear green macs.'
The little frog shouted:
'What are you talking about?
There isn't even the tiniest cloud in the sky,
I'll look silly walking around like that.'
But her mother said: 'Be quiet,
you can carry it easily enough –
and what if it looks like rain, what will you do then?
You must always think ahead.'
And so they bought the green mac.
But from that day on the little frog was naughty,
she would only go out

when it looked like rain.
It was too much to put up with.
Her father said: 'Stay at home,
it's going to rain buckets.'
But the naughty little frog answered:
'What have I got that mac for, then?'
And she went quite calmly out,
She went quite calmly for a walk.
And people who saw her go by
said: 'Froggy sort of weather, isn't it?'

A home for six thousand alarm-clocks

Imagine a little blue alarm-clock who hadn't ever woken anybody up – he could hardly wait for the chance. He simply couldn't think of anything but ringing his alarm, his head was full to bursting with it, and he asked everybody he met what it was really like to ring.

In the end a gentleman bought him. He wound him up and set his alarm for six o'clock precisely. As you might guess, the alarm-clock didn't get any sleep that night. He was so excited that he counted the minutes away, imagining how marvellous it was going to be when his alarm went off.

'I'll have to be right on time,' he said to himself. He was pleased as punch to be behaving just like a grown-up alarm-clock.

It was five o'clock already. Then it was five to six – only a few minutes to go. 'Here we go,' the alarm-clock said at last, and he cleared his throat and sounded the alarm.

It sounded like fifteen alarm-clocks, like the Gulf Stream, four sailing-boats, nine larks, and a quarter of a kilo of frozen fruit put together! It really was marvellous, for all he had was a little voice, a lot of courage, and a willing heart.

But what do you think of this: suddenly *he got a box on the ears bigger than a salad bowl!*

He was very upset; it was no fun for him any more. How else would he feel? A box on the ears is a box on the ears, after all. Would you like to be treated like that?

All day long he kept thinking about it, turning things over in his mind. In the end he told himself: 'Perhaps I didn't wake him on time. People are particular about being on time.' So he decided to be more on time.

Well, he felt rather nervous the whole night long, and in the morning he was so anxious that he could hardly breathe. But he set off his alarm right on time – *nobody* could have been more on time.

But what do you think of this: *he got a box on the ears like a rocking-chair!*

He was very upset about it, of course, but he was beginning to get curious too. It wouldn't do for him just to wonder *what* was happening, he wanted to see clearly *why*. He loved waking people up and he would have given anything to be able to, but having his ears boxed spoiled everything.

So he thought it over, and said to himself: 'I musn't be too much on time. Perhaps the gentleman wants to sleep longer – there's nothing wrong with that. He has every right to. I'll wake him a quarter of an hour later.' And the following morning he woke him up at a quarter past six.

But what do you think of this: *he got a box on the ears like a vegetable stall!*

'Huh!' he said to himself. 'If I wake him on time, I get a box on the ears. If I wake him later, I get a box on the ears. I'll wake him a little earlier – this gentleman seems to be an early bird. I just don't understand people.' And the following morning he set off the alarm at a quarter to six.

But what do you think of this: *he got a box on the ears like the Statue of Liberty!*

By now the alarm-clock was absolutely desperate. He felt like crying, and he was afraid to ring at all. He was so desperate that he couldn't help but come to a desperate decision: he wouldn't ring at all.

And indeed, the following morning there wasn't a peep from him. He just kept silent and waited.

Nothing happened. All was quiet, and the alarm-clock felt as if a weight had been taken off his shoulders. 'At last,' he thought, 'I've solved the problem!' And he rubbed his hands, feeling pleased with himself. But suddenly at half-past eight, for no reason at all, *he got a box on the ears like an ice-breaker with three funnels!*

You can understand, can't you, he'd had just as much as he could take. So he picked himself up and walked out on tiptoe. To cut a long story short, he went to look around to see if there was another alarm-clock with the same problem.

His luck was in. He met an alarm-clock that was the image of himself, with a dial and hands – the only difference being that he was red all over.

'Now then, how do you get on with this waking-up business?' asked our blue alarm-clock.

'It doesn't bear thinking about,' answered the red alarm-clock. 'When I'm on time, I get a box on the ears, when I ring *later* I get a box on the ears, when I ring *earlier* I get a box on the ears, and when I don't ring at all I get a box on the ears like an ice-breaker with three funnels.'

'Well,' said the blue alarm-clock, 'it seems that we're in the same boat. Let's call all alarm-clocks together for a

council.' So they summoned all alarm-clocks to a meeting in the park at night.

Night was falling, stars were sparkling in the sky, and in the park they were standing dial to dial: six thousand alarm-clocks, waiting to see what was going to happen. You could hear the ticking as far as the town square.

When the alarm-clocks were assembled, the blue alarm-clock said: 'Stop ticking, then you can hear what I'm saying.' The alarm-clocks stopped ticking, and listened to what the blue alarm-clock had to say.

This is what he said: 'Alarm-clocks! We love to ring our alarms, and there's nothing wrong with that – we are alarm-clocks, after all. But we will not put up with having our ears boxed for no reason at all.'

'Hear, hear!' shouted the alarm-clocks. 'We're all fed up to the cogs with it!'

'Alarm-clocks!' continued the blue alarm-clock. 'We have a fine job to do. Anyone who has rung his alarm once will know that there is nothing finer in the world. But this boxing of ears spoils everything. I propose we go to some place where we can ring *without* being boxed on the ears.'

'Yes, let's go!' the alarm-clocks cried. 'Don't let's waste words any more.'

And they started to tick again, and they walked and walked until they reached the blue sea. Then they boarded a ship, and they sailed until they reached an island where there was just room for six thousand alarm-clocks.

'Alarm-clocks!' said the blue alarm-clock. 'Here you see our Promised Land, here we can ring from morning till night without waking anybody.'

The alarm-clocks were very excited. They shouted

'hooray!' and started to ring, and they rang without stopping, each one ringing just as he liked. And so suddenly, in the middle of the blue sea, there was a little island filled with the silvery sound of ringing. It was wonderful!

How can I describe it? It was like a sea full of Gulf Streams, flocks of larks and sailing-boats, and lots of frozen fruit *all put together*.

The giraffe who was no good at gym

When the giraffe went to school
she used to get ten out of ten in maths and reading,
but she always got nought in gym
because she couldn't turn somersaults.
Try and try as she might, she couldn't do a somersault at
    all.
She was very unhappy about it.
Everybody told her:
'This is how you do it, like this,
look, it's quite easy.'
But the giraffe never managed it,
she didn't know what to do with her neck.
The teacher would say to her:
'Oh, giraffe, giraffe, what a clumsy thing you are,
you're going to get a fine report –
what will your parents say?'
And the giraffe cried so much
that anybody passing by
thought it was raining.
When the school year ended
and the reports were given out,
the giraffe really had got nought out of ten in gym,

and she cried even more than before.
When she came home
her mum and dad asked her
what was the matter,
and the giraffe confessed she'd got nought out of ten in
     gym.
Mum and Dad said nothing.
They just went into the next room
and talked for a long time in there.
When they came back
they brought their own old school reports with them.
And when the young giraffe looked at them she found that
they had got nought out of ten in gym as well.

The snowmen and the miracle of life

The sun has a lot of work to do: it wakes people up, it dries the washing, it never stops working. Without the sun, the peonies wouldn't grow, and the redcurrants wouldn't ripen. The sun produces life; but for some, the sun produces death. You may not believe it, but you just ask the snowmen. Life is a complicated thing, and happiness for one person means unhappiness for another. Unfortunately, that's how things are, and there's nothing we can do about it, except put up with it.

But one day along came two snowmen who had no intention of accepting things as they were. Somewhere they had heard about flowers, cherries, and apricots, and they longed to see each of them. In all their lives they had known nothing but snow and dark, black tree-trunks. As far as they knew, butterflies didn't exist, except in the imagination.

Well, they thought about it, and decided they would find out for themselves. To cut a long story short, they made up their minds to live on till the summer, whatever happened. You have to admit, this was very enterprising of them. They weren't going to spend their lives doing nothing, like most people you see.

The average age of a snowman is about three months because, when the sun gets warmer, for the snowman it means the end. So the two snowmen said to themselves: 'Before the sun gets warmer, we must disappear.' And so one day the two of them called on the manager of the ice-factory.

It was quite a surprise for him, but he just acted as if he were giving the matter serious thought. 'Why not?' he said to himself. 'There's room enough here, after all.' He really admired the ambition of the two snowmen.

So the snowmen moved into the dark store-room where big blocks of ice were stored. They got rather bored, but they said to each other: 'Well, patience bears fruit. At any rate, we'll see what the fruit looks like.' And while they waited, they talked to each other about incidents in their life: they had seen two crows and four children, and that seemed like a miracle to them. When life gets dull, you see, some people think back to faraway lands, others think back to two old crows.

But one day, the manager came in with his torch. 'Come on,' he said, 'things have started outside, summer is in full swing.'

The snowmen's hearts were nearly bursting as they went outside. Suddenly they felt the gust of hot air, and turned their eyes towards the light. They recognized the trees, covered with green leaves. They saw yellow tulips and white roses, redcurrants, pink raspberries, and lots of blue butterflies. The snowmen stood in the midst of all this splendour, unable to utter a single word.

But slowly they began to melt. The manager didn't know what to say; he understood how emotional they felt. Swallows were flying around them, and the manager said:

'That's a swallow, she comes from faraway lands.' The snowmen looked at the swallow as if she were a miracle, and the swallow looked at the two shrinking snowmen as if they were ghosts. She had never seen anything like it before, and she wondered if she was going crazy.

Everything around the two snowmen was growing, but they were getting smaller and smaller. Life really is beyond belief, and the two small snowmen were amazed at the swallow and at all those unbelievable miracles around them. They burst into tears, and the more tears they shed, the smaller they became, till in the end the manager couldn't see anybody; just a few tears sparkling in the grass, like precious stones.